2 adventures #1

DOUBLE TROUBLE

Ray hung up the phone and walked back to the counter.

"Who was on the phone?" asked Reggie.

Ray didn't look happy. "Heads up, you guys. I'm afraid I've got some bad news."

Everyone stopped eating their pancakes.

"Tito's got the flu," Ray continued. "He can't come into work today."

"That's too bad," said Otto. "I guess he won't get to see me win my trophy."

"Yes, he can," said Twister. "I'll get a video of you winning your trophy."

"I'm sorry, Otto, but that's not gonna happen," said Ray. "There aren't going to be any trophies. I'm going to need your help here today. A big crowd is gonna turn up for the contest. I can't handle it alone."

"What? I have to miss the contest?" cried Otto.

"There'll be other contests," said Ray.

Otto didn't know what to do. He couldn't miss this contest. "Dad, can't you find someone else?" he asked. "I'm skating better than I ever have. I have a shot at winning! I could—"

Ray held up his hand. "Otto, I said I'm sorry. You and your sister are the only people who know what to do around here."

Double Trouble

Based on the TV series *Nickelodeon Rocket Power*™,
created by Klasky Csupo, Inc. as seen on Nickelodeon®

SIMON SPOTLIGHT
An imprint of Simon & Schuster Children's Publishing Division
1230 Avenue of the Americas, New York, New York 10020

Manufactured in the United States of America

First Edition
2 4 6 8 10 9 7 5 3

ISBN 0-689-84555-3

Library of Congress Catalog Card Number: 2001090076

Rocket Power Adventures #1

Double Trouble

by Steven Banks

based on the teleplays by
Scott Gray, Michael Bloom,
and Andy McElfresh

Simon Spotlight/Nickelodeon

New York   London   Toronto   Sydney   Singapore

story #1
OTTOMOBILE

chapter 1

"I'm gonna tear this half-pipe up, baby!" shouted Otto Rocket.

The Madtown Skateboard Championship had just begun. It was the biggest, coolest, most wicked skate event of the year!

Otto was waiting for the "okay" sign to race down the half-pipe ramp. Below him hundreds of people watched. Otto's sister, Reggie, and his friend Sam were in the stands cheering him on.

"Go, Rocket boy!" shouted Reggie.

"Go for the gold, Otto!" yelled Sam.

Standing on top of the half-pipe with Otto was Twister, his friend. As usual Twister had his trusty video camera at his side, filming everything.

"You're the best, Otto, nobody can beat you," he said.

Then the announcer gave the "okay" sign, and Otto raced down the ramp.

"Yeah, baby! Rocket boy rules!" he shouted.

Otto sailed down one side of the ramp and then raced up the other. He did turns and flips and went upside down twice! He sailed through the air like he was flying! It was awesome.

Reggie nudged Sam, "I think he's gonna win it this year."

"I know he is!" Sam agreed.

Otto finished his routine with some super-hard moves and then waved to the crowd.

The announcer's voice came over the loudspeaker: "With that spectacular run and an average score of 9.3, Otto Rocket takes the lead!"

The crowd cheered.

"Way to go, Rocket boy!" shouted Sam.

"Yeah, Otto!" yelled Reggie.

Otto had half an hour to kill before round two started.

"I feel the need to feed," announced Otto. "Let's hit the Shore Shack for some pancakes!"

At the Shore Shack, Otto, Twister, Reggie, and Sam sat at the counter. Otto and Reggie's dad, Ray, was at the grill cooking pancakes for breakfast.

"Otto, dude, you were awesome in the first round!" said Twister.

"Yeah, Rocket boy, you nailed every

move with style," agreed Reggie.

"I've never seen you bust bigger air," Sam said with a smile. "I would have busted something else!"

"I have to admit it, you're all right," said Otto. "That trophy's as good as mine and I know just where I'm gonna put it." Otto pointed to a shelf way up high over the grill. "Right there, where everybody can see it!"

"Coming at ya!" said Ray as he set a huge stack of pancakes down on the counter. "You guys talking about the Madtown skate contest?"

"Yeah, Dad," said Reggie reaching for the syrup.

"It's gonna be a *big* day today," said Ray.

"It sure is," agreed Otto, thinking about his trophy.

"No, I mean it's gonna be a very big day here for *me*," said Ray.

Otto looked up, confused. How could it possibly be a big day for his dad?

"Why?" he asked.

"Because—," Ray began.

Just then the phone rang. Ray went to answer it while everybody ate their pancakes.

"These are good, man!" said Twister, his mouth full.

"Your dad's a great cook," added Sam.

Otto nodded. "I'm gonna need a lot of energy to win that trophy, so I'm gonna eat ten!"

Ray picked up the phone. "Hello. Ray Rocket speaking."

It was Tito, Ray's friend and the cook at the Shack.

"This is your best friend in the world, Tito Earl Anthony Kewaholo Makani, Jr. calling."

"Aloha, Tito. What's up?" asked Ray.

Tito sneezed into his phone. "AH-CHOO!"

"You sound terrible!" said Ray.

"Man, I'm sick," said Tito. "Sick as a dog!"

"What kind of dog?" asked Ray.

"A dog who's got the flu," said Tito. "Listen, bro, I can't come in to work today."

"You can't? But we're gonna be super busy! The beach is gonna be jammed. A big crowd is gonna be here for the skate championship."

"I know, bro," said Tito. "But do you want me sneezing on the customers?" asked Tito.

Ray shook his head. "No. I don't think the customers would like that."

Tito sneezed again. "AH-CHOO!"

"You better stay in bed, man. Don't worry, Tito. We'll handle everything down here. Do you need anything?"

"No, thanks, cuz," replied Tito. "I got a big pot of chicken mango-ball soup. Just like mama used to make. I'll see you tomorrow. Aloha!"

Ray hung up the phone and walked back to the counter.

"Who was on the phone?" asked Reggie.

Ray didn't look happy. "Heads up, you guys. I'm afraid I've got some bad news."

Everyone stopped eating their pancakes.

"Tito's got the flu," Ray continued. "He can't come in to work today."

"That's too bad," said Otto. "I guess he won't get to see me win my trophy."

"Yes, he can," said Twister. "I'll get a video of you winning your trophy."

"I'm sorry, Otto, but that's not gonna happen," said Ray. "There aren't going to be any trophies. I'm going to need your help here today. A big crowd is gonna turn up for the contest. I can't handle it alone."

"What? I have to miss the contest?" cried Otto.

"There'll be other contests," said Ray.

"Otto, I feel your pain," said Reggie, trying to comfort her brother.

"Reggie, I need you to work too," said Ray.

"I have to work?" cried Reggie. "Hey, Dad, there are child-labor laws, you know."

Sam cleared his throat. "Actually, Reggie, the Fair Labor Standards Act of 1938 doesn't cover immediate family members."

"What does that mean?" demanded Reggie.

"It means your dad can make you work," said Sam.

"When I'm president of the United

States, that is the first law I'm gonna change!" said Reggie.

Otto didn't know what to do. He couldn't miss this contest. "Dad, can't you find someone else?" he asked. "I'm skating better than I ever have. I have a shot at winning! I could—"

Ray held up his hand. "Otto, I said I'm sorry. You and your sister are the only people who know what to do around here."

"I know what to do around here," Sam chimed in.

"Sam, all you know how to do around here is *eat*," said Reggie.

"But, Dad! I gotta be in this contest!" insisted Otto.

"I don't have time to argue," said Ray. "Reggie, please start setting up the tables. Otto, you do the dishes. I'll do everything else."

Ray walked into the kitchen.

Reggie looked over at Otto. She had never seen him look so bummed. "Dad needs us, Otto," she said. "Forget the competition."

"Forget the competition?" cried Otto. "No way! I'm winning that trophy!"

"You can't win that trophy if you're not in the contest," said Sam.

"I'm gonna be in that contest! And I'm gonna win that trophy," said Otto.

"The only contest you're gonna win today is the Best Dishwasher contest," said Reggie, throwing her brother a dishtowel.

"Wait a minute!" said Otto. "Reggie, can you cover for me? Do all the work yourself? Please?"

"That's impossible! There's too much to do," said Reggie. "I only have two hands! What do you think I am, an *octopus*?"

Sam cleared his throat. "Uh . . . I can help."

Twister put his hand on Reggie's shoulder. "Come on, Reggie, you gotta cover for Otto. He *is* your brother."

Reggie looked at Twister. "Would you do this for your brother?" she asked.

"Which one?" Twister asked.

"Any of them!" said Reggie.

"No way," replied Twister. "'Cause I know they wouldn't do it for me. But if Otto was my brother, I'd cover for him!"

Reggie turned to Otto. "Dad wouldn't have asked us if he didn't really need us. We *are* the only ones that know what to do around here."

"*Anyone* can do dishes," said Otto. "It's not exactly brain surgery!"

Sam tapped Reggie on the shoulder. "Excuse me, I have brains. I know how to wash dishes!"

But Reggie wasn't listening to Sam. Instead she handed Otto a dirty dish and said, "Forget it, Otto. Let's get to work."

"But I *have* to be in this contest!" cried Otto.

"Will someone listen to me?" yelled Sam. "I am talking over here! I said I can fill in! I can do dishes!"

Otto looked at Sam. "Hmmm . . . well, the skate rounds are short," he said. "What if I skate *and* work? Sam could fill in until I get back."

Reggie shook her head, "If Dad thinks you're working and you're not, he'll wig out! The next time you'll be allowed to skate in a contest will be in college!"

"But if Dad doesn't find out, there's no problem," said Otto. "C'mon, Reg!"

"Do it for the Otto-man!" said Twister.

Reggie sighed, "Okay. But you owe me a *HUGE* favor for doing this, Otto!"

"Name it," said Otto as he strapped on his helmet.

Reggie started to think. This had to be one of the biggest favors of all time. "Okay, I got it. If I do this for you, then you gotta clean and lube my skates."

"No problem," said Otto.

Reggie crossed her arms and smiled, "For the next *two* years."

"Two years!" shouted Otto. "That's . . . that's . . ."

Sam quickly did the math in his head. "That's 730 days."

But Otto knew he had no choice. He *had* to be in this skateboard competition.

"Okay, Reggie, I'll do it!" he said.

Then Otto grabbed his skateboard. "All right! I am out of here! See you after the second round!"

Reggie yelled to Otto as he and Twister skated away, "This better work! 'Cause if it doesn't, we're in big trouble!"

"It will!" shouted Otto over his shoulder

as he skated away. "Trust me!"

"I hate it when he says that," said Reggie. And then she turned to Sam. "Okay, let's get to work."

Sam grabbed an apron. "All right! I'm ready! Where's my sponge? This is gonna be so cool!"

chapter 2

Otto and Twister got back to the contest just as the second round was about to begin.

"The crowd is stoked here in Ocean Shores," said Twister, pretending to be an announcer. "The legendary Otto Rocket, local mega-skateboard freak, is getting ready to rock out." Twister aimed his camera at Otto. "Otto, how about a word for the folks at home?"

"Don't bug me right now, Twister," said

Otto. "I'm trying to concentrate!"

Otto was thinking about which moves he was going to do when it was his turn. Each move had to be done perfectly. No mess-ups. No mistakes.

Twister kept on talking and filming, "The question on everyone's mind is, will young Otto make all the right moves? Will he make any mistakes? Will he crush the competition?"

Otto pushed Twister's camera out of his face. "Twister! I'm gonna crush *you* if you don't stop bothering me and get out of my way!"

Just then the announcer's voice came over a loudspeaker: "And now, our next contestant is making his second run of the day. Here's the current leader and local favorite, Otto Rocket!"

The crowd cheered.

"No prisoners, dude!" shouted Twister.

"Go for it, my friend!" He knew Otto could do it.

Otto gave the crowd a thumbs-up and pushed off down the ramp.

He raced down one side and back up the other. But he was going too fast! He had pushed off too hard, and as he flew up into the air, he realized that he was too high and that he couldn't turn.

He fell down hard!

BAM!

"Ow! That's gotta hurt!" shouted the announcer. "Young Rocket's going to need to do something really spectacular to make up for that mistake! This could cost him the championship!"

Otto stood up. Nothing was broken, but a lot of things hurt. Still, he knew what he had to do. He had to get back on that skateboard and ride again!

"Prepare to witness some totally

outrageous moves, sports fans!" he cried. "Wait till the next round! You'll see I have not yet begun to skate!"

🚀 🚀 🚀

Back at the Shore Shack, Sam was in the kitchen staring at a huge pile of dirty dishes. The pile went all the way to the ceiling. Reggie was at the grill flipping hamburgers.

"Hey, Reggie," yelled Sam. "Let me cook burgers. I'm really good with a spatula! I swear!"

Reggie didn't turn around to see what Sam was doing. She was too busy cooking. "Look, Sammy, we *all* started out doing dishes," she said. "You gotta work your way up from the bottom."

Sam looked at the stack of dishes. "From the bottom? Really?" he asked. "Okay." Then he reached for a dish on the *bottom* of the stack. The pile of dishes began to wobble back and forth. Just then Reggie turned around and saw what Sam was doing.

"Sam! No!" she screamed.

But it was too late.

CRASH!

The noise was so loud you could practically hear it all the way up at the skating competition.

Ray was waiting on a table when he heard the crash. "What is going on back there, Rocket girl?" he shouted.

Reggie poked her head out from the kitchen, "Nothing, Dad! We're just doing the dishes!"

"It sounds like you're *breaking* the dishes," said Ray.

Reggie turned back to Sam. "Sammy, you better clean up those dishes now!"

"Sorry, Reggie, but you told me to start from the bottom," Sam tried to explain.

"Never mind, just clean them up!" she said. Then she looked out the door at all the customers lining up. She had never seen it so busy.

Otto better get back here as fast as he can! she thought with a frown.

🚀 🚀 🚀

Meanwhile, back at the half-pipe ramp, it was the third round in the competition. Otto was doing better than he had done in the last round. In fact, he was doing some of the most amazing moves he had ever done in his life. He had never gone so high or so fast and he had never done so many turns and twists. When he finished his routine, the crowd went wild.

"Ladies and gentlemen, you have just witnessed one of the most amazing exhibitions and comebacks in Ocean Shores' skating history!" shouted the announcer.

Twister was up on top of the half-pipe with Otto. He shook Otto's hand. "Man, that was the total bomb! You are the man among men!"

"Thanks, Twister," said Otto. "Now I gotta jam out of here! Reggie's gonna whomp me big time if I don't get back to the Shore Shack!"

"But don't you want to see your scores?" asked Twister.

"I don't have time!" said Otto as he raced off.

But Twister wasn't in such a hurry. He aimed his video camera at the scoreboard and watched Otto's scores come up:

Ten. Ten. Ten. Ten. Ten. Perfect scores all the way.

"Otto!" yelled Twister after his friend. "You made the semifinals!"

Otto smiled, turned around, and gave Twister a thumbs-up as he skated off.

Meanwhile, the Shore Shack was getting even busier. All the tables were filled and even more people were waiting. Ray was cooking the food as fast as he could.

All the customers were yelling:

"I want a burger!"

"I want two burgers!"

"I want five burgers!"

Reggie could hardly write down the orders fast enough. "Rocket girl! We need more burgers!" he yelled.

"I'm on my way, Dad!" shouted Reggie. As she went to the door she turned to Sam. "We need more burger patties from the freezer, Sammy!"

"You got it!" said Sam, and he raced off to the freezer.

Sam opened the big silver door to the freezer. He could feel the cold air as soon as he opened it. He stepped inside and looked up at the shelves above him.

"Wow! This is awesome!" he exclaimed.

It was so cold that frost came out of his mouth. He looked up at the ice-cream shelf, filled with rows and rows of different kinds of ice cream. "There must be thirty-two flavors in here!" he said to himself. "I could stay in here forever!"

Just then the door closed behind him and the lights went out. Sam tugged at the handle, but it didn't budge.

He was trapped!

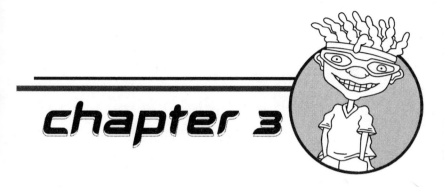

chapter 3

Otto raced as fast as he could to get back to the Shore Shack, but the boardwalk was jammed with people. He had to dodge in and out of tourists. "Coming through!" he yelled. "Excuse me! I got places to go! People to see!"

When he got to the Shore Shack he saw the huge crowd. Ray was in front, bringing food to people and trying to clean up dirty tables at the same time. Otto decided to sneak around the back, where they kept the trash cans, so his dad wouldn't see him.

"REGGIE!" shouted Ray inside.

Reggie popped her head out of the kitchen. "Yeah, Dad?"

"I need these tables cleaned now! Where is that brother of yours?"

"Uh . . . what brother?" asked Reggie.

"I don't have time to play games! Tell him to get out here!" shouted Ray.

Just then there was a huge *CRASH* from the back of the shack. It sounded like all the trash barrels had fallen over!

"I think he's out back taking out the trash," said Reggie.

"Well, I'm going to go get him," said Ray.

"Wait!" shouted Reggie. But it was too late. Ray was already on his way to the garbage cans.

Ray opened the back door and there was Otto, lying on the ground, covered in garbage. A trash can lid was sitting on top of his head. He was covered in half-eaten hot dog buns, old hamburger patties, bits of french fries, onion rings, and tomatoes.

"Hi, Dad," said Otto cheerily. "How's it going?"

"I like your enthusiasm, Otto, but I need you clearing tables, pronto!"

"You got it, Dad!" said Otto.

"Clean yourself up first. You got a tomato in your ear."

As Ray walked away, Reggie helped Otto up. "You *gotta* stay, Otto. The place is packed!"

"I can't stay!" cried Otto. "I just skated the best I've ever skated. I made the semifinals! I'm in the lead!"

"Forget it, Otto!" said Reggie. "There is no way you're going back. We really need you here. This place is crazy!"

"Sorry, Reg. I can't hear you," said Otto

with a grin. "I got a tomato in my ear."

Reggie pulled the tomato out of Otto's ear. "Otto! We are overrun!"

"*Run?* Did you say *run?*" asked Otto. "You're right! I should *run*. Back to the contest!" And with that, Otto skated away.

Reggie couldn't believe Otto was leaving. "Hey, get back here!" she yelled.

But Otto was too far away to hear her. He had already disappeared into the crowd.

"You'd *better* get that trophy," Reggie muttered under her breath.

🚀 🚀 🚀

Back at the contest, the announcer was speaking into his microphone. "We are ready to begin the semifinal round. Will all the semifinalists please report to the half-pipe?"

Twister was looking for Otto, but he couldn't find him anywhere. Otto was going to miss the round! Twister aimed his video camera around the pier. "Sports fans, this looks bad! And I'm talking mega bad! Otto Rocket, everyone's favorite, is nowhere to be seen! The semifinals are only seconds away! Will he make it back in time? Will he win the championship?"

🚀 🚀 🚀

Back at the Shore Shack the customers were getting angry.

"Waitress!" shouted a woman. "I ordered my burger medium and this is cooked medium-well!"

"Sorry, ma'am," apologized Reggie.

"Waitress!" yelled a tall man. "I need a cup of ice!"

"Coming right up, sir!" called Reggie.

"Waitress!" called a little boy. "My hamburger is cold!"

"Waitress!" shouted an old man. "My ice cream is hot!"

Ray stuck his head out the window. "Reggie! Where is that brother of yours? We need all the help we can get!"

Forget about my brother. Where's Sammy? Reggie wondered to herself.

At the skate championship, Twister was still shouting from the top of the half-pipe, "Otto! Where are you?"

"This is the *last* call for Otto Rocket!" warned the announcer. "If he does not show up now, he will be disqualified from the contest!"

Suddenly Otto came up the ramp riding his skateboard.

"I'm here! I'm here!" he shouted. He was still covered in ice-cream wrappers, hamburger buns, and soggy french fries.

Twister breathed a sigh of relief.

Otto waved to the crowd, who cheered.

"Ot-to! Ot-to! Ot-to!" they chanted.

Otto raced down the half-pipe.

"Who's the man?!" he shouted.

Then he flipped over and hit the other side of the half-pipe. The crowd cheered again.

"Who's the king?" he yelled as he turned and sailed down the other side.

Otto was so high up he could actually see the Shore Shack. Ray was standing on a table trying to calm down the angry crowd. Reggie was running around as fast as she could trying to serve people.

Uh-oh! Who's in trouble? thought Otto.

When he finished his routine, Twister continued filming him.

"Way to go, Rocket boy!" he yelled. "You're gonna make the finals!"

"If I don't get back to the Shack, I'm not going to make anything!" shouted Otto as he raced off.

chapter 4

Back at the Shore Shack all the customers were yelling at Reggie.

"We want food! We want service! We want our bill!"

Reggie couldn't take it any longer. She jumped up on top of a table and screamed at the top of her lungs, "People! Listen up!"

The crowd stopped yelling.

"If you want my attention," she said, "*Say* it, don't *scream* it! I am working as hard and as fast as I can! You may now continue eating your meals, but do it QUIETLY!"

The crowd sat in stunned silence.

"Yes, miss," someone finally whispered.

Ray helped his daughter get down off the table. "Nice work, kiddo," he said. "But you gotta work on your people skills a little."

"Pop, sometimes a girl's gotta do what a girl's gotta do. It isn't always pretty, but it gets the job done!"

"Whatever you say, Rocket girl," said Ray. "But your brother seems to have disappeared *again!* Do you know where he is?"

"Hey, Reg, I'm back," said Otto as he calmly walked out of the kitchen.

"Back from *where?*" asked Ray.

Twister burst into the restaurant. He was so excited. "Otto made the finals!" he shouted.

"The finals?" asked Ray. "What finals?"

"Ooops," said Twister. "Something tells me I shouldn't have said that."

Otto looked to Reggie for help. She shook her head. "You're on your own, Rocket boy."

Ray looked at Otto. "Son? Were you in the skateboard contest?"

"Uh . . . yeah," said Otto softly.

Ray shook his head. "Otto, I asked for your help. I can't believe you would be so . . . so . . ." He was trying to think of the right word.

"Irresponsible? Selfish? Immature?" suggested Reggie.

Ray turned to Reggie, "Thank you, but I can handle this on my own. I do have one question for you though, Reg," said Ray. "Did you know about your brother's little scheme? That he was blowing us off all along?"

"Well, I . . . ," Reggie began nervously.

"Thanks for the help, Reggie!" said Otto. "You can forget about me cleaning your skates!"

"Cleaning your skates?" asked Ray. "Reggie, did you make a deal behind my back?"

"Well, you see, Dad . . . ," Reggie started to explain.

"You both know better than to lie to me," said Ray disappointedly.

Otto felt terrible. "Sorry, Dad," he said as he hung his head.

"I'm sorry too," said Reggie, who felt pretty bad herself.

Then Otto looked up. "But I *did* make the finals, Dad."

"I don't care if you made the Olympic team!" said Ray.

"Mr. Rocket," said Twister, trying to be as helpful as he could, "I don't think they have skateboarding in the Olympics."

"Twister, I think we can handle this on our own," whispered Reggie.

"Look, Dad, I know I should be helping you," said Otto. "But I made the finals, and I really need to get back to finish competing. I'm gonna leave it up to you. You can let me skate in the finals or you can make me help out here. You decide."

Ray sighed. "Otto, I think you should help here."

Otto's mouth dropped open. "And miss the finals?!" he cried. "But, Dad, this was my day! I could've been somebody! I could've been a champion! I—"

"You didn't let me finish," said Ray. "I *think* you should help here, but I'm going to let you skate in the contest."

Otto looked up, "You are? Really?"

"I'll figure out some sort of *other* punishment later," said Ray.

"Dad, you're the best!" said Otto.

"You're going to want to remember that you said that when you're being punished," said Ray.

"Thanks, Dad," said Otto. Then he jumped on his skateboard and turned to everyone. "It's trophy time!"

Reggie watched as Otto sped off. "You let him off too easy, Dad."

"Don't worry, Reg. He's not going to get off easy," said Ray. "And neither are you."

Just then the customers started shouting again:

"I want ice cream!"

"I ordered onion rings, not french fries!"

"Okay, Rocket girl," said Ray. "We gotta get back to work! We have customers to serve."

"Okay, Dad," said Reggie. "Hey, at least we have Sammy to help. Wait a second, where *is* Sam? The last time I saw him he was going to get something out of the . . . oh, no . . . out of the freezer!"

Ray and Reggie ran to the kitchen.

"I hope he didn't turn into a iceberg!" said Reggie as she opened the freezer door.

Sam was covered in ice. His face was blue and his teeth were chattering.

"I-I-I-I-I-I-I-I—," he said.

"What is it, Sammy?" asked Reggie. "What are you trying to say?"

Sam finally spit it out: "I-I-Ice cream, anyone?" he asked as he held out a carton of mint chocolate chip. "I f-f-figured since I was t-t-t-trapped in here I might as well enjoy myself!"

chapter 5

Later, after Reggie and Ray had defrosted Sam, the three of them managed to serve all the customers at the Shore Shack.

And Otto won his trophy.

When the last customer left the Shack, Ray made hot-fudge sundaes for everyone except Sam. He had had enough ice cream for the day. Even Tito, who was feeling better, came down to make sure everything was okay.

"This sundae sure makes me feel a whole

lot better, bruddah!" said Tito happily.

"Glad you like it, Tito," said Ray.

Just as Twister, Tito, and Ray were finishing their sundaes, Twister asked, "Hey, do you think Otto and Reggie want sundaes too?"

"Not right now," said Ray. "I think they're gonna be busy for a long time."

Meanwhile, back in the kitchen, piled high next to Reggie and Otto was the biggest stack of dishes either one of them had ever seen.

"How long do you think it will take us to wash all these dishes?" asked Otto.

"About two years," said Reggie.

Then they both looked up at the top shelf, over the sink, where Otto's trophy for first place sat.

"Nice job, Otto," said Reggie.

"I couldn't have done it without you, Reg!"

Reggie looked at the huge pile of dishes. "I sure wish you could have. Now, keep washing!"

story #2
DOWN THE DRAIN

chapter 1

"Wow! I can't believe it!" shouted Otto Rocket.

Otto and his friends, Twister and Sam, were bouncing up and down on Otto's trampoline. Otto and Twister were bouncing so high they could see over the tall hedges into Otto's neighbors', the Stimpletons, backyard. The Stimpletons had a big, beautiful pool in their backyard.

Every time Otto bounced up on the trampoline he could see Mr. and Mrs.

Stimpleton showing his sister, Reggie, around the pool.

"This is too good to be true!" yelled Twister as he bounced up and down and saw Reggie too.

Sam was confused. "What's too good to be true?" he asked. "Is this your first time on a trampoline, Twister?"

"No way! Me and this trampoline go way back," said Twister. "Check out the action next door!"

Sam tried to bounce high enough to see over the hedges but it was a little too scary for him. "What is it?" he asked.

"Bail out and you'll see!" said Otto as he bounced off the trampoline and landed on the grass.

Twister did the same, landing next to Otto.

"Come on, Squid-man. Dismount!" called Otto.

Sam slowly stopped bouncing and then carefully climbed off the trampoline.

Otto, Twister, and Sam poked their heads through the hedges to get a better look at what was going on next door.

Reggie was holding a big, thick book called *How to Take Care of Your Pool in 1,000 Easy Lessons*.

"Reggie," said Mr. Stimpleton, "I'm leaving you in charge while we're away. So pay careful attention!"

"I will, Mr. Stimpleton," replied Reggie.

"This is the most important part of your house-sitting job," said Mr. Stimpleton as he pointed at the pool. "Behold, the glorious Stimpleton in-ground aquatic recreation center!"

Mrs. Stimpleton shook her head, "Oh, Merv, it's just a pool!"

Otto, Twister, and Sam couldn't contain their excitement anymore.

The three boys popped through the hedge.

"Hi, Mr. and Mrs. Stimpleton!" said Otto.

"Quiet, whippersnapper!" ordered Mr. Stimpleton. "I'm giving your sister some very important information here." He turned to Reggie, "Now, where was I?"

"You were at the pool," said Reggie.

"Right!" said Mr. Stimpleton. "Glad to see you're paying attention. Now, the pool is comprised of 16,500 liters of anti-bacterial chlorinated water, precisely heated to sixty-eight degrees."

Otto turned to Sam and Twister, "Can you two say 'pool party'?"

"Pool party!" shouted Sam and Twister.

Mr. Stimpleton turned around angrily. "Pool party?" He turned to his wife. "Violet! That is exactly why I have extreme reservations about leaving these hooligans in charge of *my* precious pool!"

Mrs. Stimpleton shook her head. "Oh, calm down, Merv! Reggie will do a wonderful job taking care of everything. The Rockets are just like family to us."

Mrs. Stimpleton leaned down and gave Otto a big pinch on the cheek. "Right, Otto?"

Otto *hated* it when Mrs. Stimpleton did that.

Reggie gave Otto, Twister, and Sam the evil eye and pulled them aside. "Will you guys chill?"

Then Mr. Stimpleton opened the door to his pool-pump unit, which looked like a little house. Inside was a computer screen and keyboard. "Now, pay attention, Reggie," he said. "The pool is controlled by what we experts call a C.P.U."

"That means Central Processing Unit," said Sam.

"Shhhh!" said Reggie.

Mr. Stimpleton continued. "This also controls the house lights, the stereo, the air conditioner, the garage door, the windows—"

"Okay, Merv!" said Mrs. Stimpleton. "It controls everything! Now come along, we have to be in Mt. Shasta by noon or we'll be late for your first anger-management class."

"Then let me finish!" cried Mr. Stimpleton. "If Reggie is going to watch our house for a week, she has to be prepared!"

"Don't worry, sir," said Reggie, "I've got everything totally under control."

Otto stepped forward. "Everything's gonna be fine, Mr. S! Remember my motto: 'Trust in Otto!'"

"I wouldn't trust you as far as I could throw you!" said Mr. Stimpleton.

"Don't worry. I've got Otto totally

under my control too," said Reggie.

Sam leaned closer to the computer. "Wow! This baby's got an ultra-super-megabyte with hydrochips!"

"Back off, whiz kid!" said Mr. Stimpleton, pulling Sam away from the expensive machine.

"Merv, we are going! *Now!*" called Mrs. Stimpleton from the car. Mr. Stimpleton and the kids walked outside to the driveway.

"And remember, kids," continued Mrs. Stimpleton, "to make your swim-time fun complete, wait an hour after you eat!"

"Yes, ma'am," said Twister.

"If we have to wait an hour, can we have something to eat now?" whispered Sam to Reggie.

"And make sure you take a shower before you go into the pool," said Mr. Stimpleton. "No dirty kids in my pool!"

Otto saluted. "Yes, sir! No dirty kids!"

As their car pulled out of the driveway, Mr. Stimpleton stuck his head out the window. "And no shenanigans!"

The kids waved to the Stimpletons as they drove away.

But Mr. Stimpleton kept yelling all the way down the block. "And no pool parties! And no food! And no toys in the pool! And no skateboards in the backyard!"

Finally the car turned the corner, and they were gone.

"Dudes—," said Twister.

"—last one in the pool skates with training wheels!" shouted Otto, finishing his friend's sentence.

chapter 2

Otto and Twister pulled off their shirts and started to run toward the pool. But Reggie jumped in front of them. "Hold it!" she yelled.

Otto and Twister came to a screeching halt.

"Were you losers in a coma just now?" she asked. "Remember what Mr. Stimpleton said? You *have* to take a shower before you get in the pool!"

Twister and Otto stopped and stared at

Reggie as if she had three heads.

"Who takes a shower before they go swimming?" asked Twister.

"Besides, if we're dirty, the pool water will clean us," added Otto.

"Sorry, guys," said Reggie. "Stimpleton's pool, Stimpleton's rules."

"That's not fair!" complained Otto.

Reggie smiled. "Gotcha!" she yelled, as she pushed them both aside, jumped off the diving board, and executed a perfect cannonball into the pool.

SPLASH!

Otto and Twister got soaked. But they didn't mind, since they were about to jump into the pool anyway. They grabbed their skateboards, raced to the diving board, and skated off into the pool.

SPLASH!

This time, Sam, who was still standing by the side of the pool, got soaked.

"Hey! That's cold!" he yelled.

"Jump in, Squid-man!" shouted Otto.

Sam backed away from the pool. "N-N-N-No, I've got to get used to it first."

"Just jump! The water's perfect!" cried Reggie.

"C'mon, Squid!" yelled Otto.

Sam looked at the water. He took a deep breath and slowly put his toe in the water. It was a bit cold.

"Hurry up!" said Twister.

Sam put his right foot in. Then he put his left foot in. Then he slowly walked down the steps into the pool.

"We said *jump!* Not *walk!*" cried Otto.

Otto and Twister swam over to Sam.

"Hey, Otto?" asked Twister. "Why is the water next to the Squid so warm?"

"Sammy! You freak!" yelled Otto.

"What?" asked Sam.

"How could you?" shouted Twister.

"How could I *what?*" asked Sam.

"Now I know why Mr. Stimpleton called you the *whiz kid!*" said Otto laughing.

Sam turned bright red. "I didn't do anything!"

"Whoever denied it supplied it!" said Twister.

Reggie shook her head. "Knock it off, guys. Give him a break."

Sam climbed out of the pool and ran over to the pump-control panel. He held his finger over the keyboard.

"Okay, you guys!" he shouted. "You know, if I wanted to, I could flush all the water in this stupid pool down the drain *right* now!"

"Don't do it, Sam!" yelled Reggie.

Otto and Twister looked at each other.

Sam was serious. "Keep making fun of me and I'll do it!" he said.

"You'll drain the pool?" asked Otto.

"Yeah," said Sam.

Otto and Twister smiled at each other.

"Sam, you're a genius!" cried Otto.

Sam was confused. He thought they'd be mad if he drained the pool. "I'm a *genius*?" he asked.

Otto nodded. "Don't you get it? Empty pool equals skateboard paradise!"

Now Sam got it. With all the water drained out, they could skateboard *inside* the swimming pool!

"Hold it!" said Reggie. "If you guys wreck the pool, Stimpleton will go totally *nuclear* on me!"

Otto jumped out of the pool. "Chill, Reg. Nothing will happen. The Sam man is an expert with this kind of stuff. Right, Sam?"

But Sam didn't hear them. He was too busy typing on the keyboard. Numbers and diagrams flashed across the screen. "If I can reverse the polarities by engaging this pump . . . then maybe . . . I can do it!"

"You can really drain the whole pool?" asked Reggie.

Sam nodded.

Reggie didn't know what to do. It *would* be fun to skate in the empty swimming pool. "Will you be able to fill it back up?" she asked.

"He can do anything," said Otto. "He's a genius!"

"Well . . . okay," said Reggie.

"Twister!" shouted Sam. "Shove that garden hose over there into the storm drain out in the driveway! I'll run the pool water out through the garden hose and empty it into the drain."

"Yes, sir!" said Twister as he grabbed the hose and ran off to find the storm drain on the other side of the hedge.

🚀 🚀 🚀

Meanwhile, as the Stimpletons were driving along Highway 1, Mr. Stimpleton turned to his wife. "Violet, I have a very bad feeling about this!"

"Stop worrying, Merv. Try to relax and enjoy yourself for once!"

"Those dang kids better not hurt my pool," grumbled Mr. Stimpleton.

"How on earth could they possibly hurt your pool?"

Mr. Stimpleton rubbed his chin. "If anyone could do it, they could!"

🚀 🚀 🚀

Back at the pool, Reggie was still worried. "Uh . . . guys, maybe we should think about this a little bit longer."

"Why *think* when we can *skate*?" asked Otto. "Don't worry! What could possibly go wrong?"

Reggie thought of about a million

things that could go wrong. For starters, she could get in trouble. BIG trouble. But Sam was smart. If anybody could do this, he could.

On the other side of the hedge, Twister quickly tossed the end of the hose into the storm drain. Then he ran back to the pool. "Hose is in the drain, General Squid-man!"

Sam rubbed his hands together and carefully typed the final instructions into the computer. "Okay, guys, here goes nothing!"

chapter 3

Otto, Twister, Reggie, and Sam waited for the pool to drain.

Nothing happened.

Twister sighed. "It sure would have been fun to skate in an empty pool."

"It might have been the greatest experience of our lives," added Otto.

"Sam, are you sure you did *everything*?" asked Reggie.

"Of course I did!" said Sam. "I entered all the information. The pool should be empty by now!" he said with a frown.

"Maybe you forgot to push the ENTER button on the computer?" asked Otto.

"It's not a button, Otto, it's a key," said Sam. "And I *know* I pushed it . . . I mean, I think I pushed it . . . I mean, I'm *almost* positive."

Sam was getting worried. Maybe he hadn't pushed it. Maybe he'd been so excited that he had forgotten.

"Push it again," said Reggie.

Sam tapped the ENTER key with his finger.

The water began to gush out of the pool!

Otto, Twister, and Reggie cheered.

"Way to go, Squid-man!"

The water was draining out of the pool fast. Little did they know, the water was so powerful that it knocked the hose *out* of the storm drain! The hose flipped up in the air and landed inside the window of Otto and Reggie's basement—and now the Rockets' basement was filling up with water! Nobody saw it happen. They were too busy watching the pool drain.

In five minutes the pool was empty.

"Wow, Sam," said Reggie. "You actually did it!"

"This is so sweet," said Twister.

Otto let out a loud whistle. "Attention, people! It is time to assume your pool party positions!"

🚀 🚀 🚀

Meanwhile, down at the pier, the Shore Shack was very quiet. There wasn't a single customer in sight. Otto and Reggie's dad, Ray, was sitting in a chair twiddling his thumbs. Tito, the cook and Ray's best friend, was sweeping the floor and whistling.

"You hungry, Ray?" asked Tito.

"No, not really."

"Are you sure? Want me to cook you up

something? Chili dog? Pastrami sandwich? Banana burger?" asked Tito.

"No, thanks," said Ray. "Man, I don't think we're gonna have any customers today, Tito."

Tito looked around at the pier. "It's a slow day, that's for sure."

Ray stood up. "I think I'm going to spend the day with my kids."

"Good idea," said Tito.

"Think you can handle the crowd down here?" asked Ray.

Tito looked around at the empty tables and chairs. "I've been training my whole life for this, bruddah."

"Great! See ya tomorrow, then," said Ray. He couldn't wait to get home.

🚀 🚀 🚀

Back at the Stimpletons', the pool party was in full force.

Otto and Twister were standing at the edge of the pool on their skateboards. Reggie was strapping on her helmet, and Sam was at the computer.

"How about some tunes, Squid?" asked Otto.

"You got it," said Sam. He typed a few words into the computer.

Four speakers popped out of the house and began to blast loud music!

Otto zipped up and down the walls of the pool on his skateboard. Twister was skateboarding and videotaping at the same time!

"Catch this, Twister!" yelled Otto. "I am about to enter the fly-right zone! Just call me Air Otto!"

Otto skated off the diving board and spun in the air. He landed in the deep end, skated across the bottom of the pool to the shallow end, and shot up the other side. He shot up so high he went over the hedges into his own backyard and crashed into the trash cans.

"Way to go, Rocket man! I got it all on video!" yelled Twister. "That was wicked decent!"

But there was no sound from the other side of the hedge.

"Otto?" called Reggie.

"Otto? You all right?" yelled Sam.

"Hey, Rocket man!" shouted Twister.

Reggie, Twister, and Sam ran to see what had happened to Otto.

Otto was lying on top of two dented trash cans, a big smile on his face. "Whoa! That was totally extreme!" he exclaimed.

Reggie's eyes widened. "What have you done?"

Otto smiled. "Well, Reg, I did an Ollie, a Butt-buster, a McTwist, a Tenth-Avenue Freezeout, up the wall into a Boned-out

Indy, and finished with a Trash Can Smasher!"

Reggie grabbed Otto and turned him around so he could see what she was seeing. "I'm not talking about skateboarding, doofus! I am talking about our basement!"

They all looked into the basement window.

"You turned our basement into an aquarium!" yelled Reggie.

It was true. The basement was filled with water. It looked like a giant fish tank. Boxes, toys, clothes, tools, an old surfboard, and a lava lamp were all floating or bobbing on the surface.

"Wow!" said Sam. "In a way, it's kind of cool!"

Reggie gave him a dirty look.

"And then, in another way, it's not so cool," said Sam.

"Your dad is gonna totally freak on you, Reggie!" said Twister.

"Freak on *me*? You're the one who put the hose in there, you little dork!" shouted Reggie.

"No, I didn't!" Twister shouted back. "I put it in the storm drain just like YOU told me to!" he said pointing at Sam.

Reggie grabbed Twister. "But it didn't go *down* the drain, Twister, it went *down* into my basement!"

"Stop yelling at me!" cried Twister. "It's the Squid's fault!"

Sam looked up. "Me? No way! I was just following orders!"

Reggie calmed down a bit. It was no use yelling at everyone. It was time to solve the problem—and fast! "Look, I don't care whose fault it was," she said. "You guys just better figure out a way to drain this place before Dad comes home from work tonight. You've got about five hours!"

Just then they heard Ray's voice coming from their front yard, "Hey, kids! I'm home!"

chapter 4

Otto, Reggie, Twister, and Sam froze in terror.

"Wow, that sounds a lot like Dad," said Otto.

"It *is* Dad!" said Reggie. "You guys go inside the house and make sure the door to the basement is closed. I'll deal with Dad!"

Otto, Twister, and Sam did what they were told and ran inside through the back door. Reggie ran around to the front of the house just as her dad was walking inside.

"Hey, Rocket girl," said Ray.

"Hey, Pops! What are you doing home?" she asked.

"Well, it was a little slow down at the Shore Shack, so I thought this would be a good day to hang out with you guys."

Reggie followed Ray inside. He was walking down the hall toward the basement door!

"Great!" said Reggie, trying to sound excited. "Why don't we go to the mall? Or the beach? Or a movie?"

"The mall's too crowded. I just came from the beach, and we've seen all the good movies," said Ray. He was getting closer to the basement door. Reggie jumped in front of him.

"Uh . . . what about going to the post office? Or the bank? Or the cleaners?" asked Reggie.

"You hate going to those places," said Ray.

"Well, maybe they got more interesting," said Reggie, still trying to sound excited.

Ray laughed and shook his head. "Not today, Reg. Do you remember that old saying? 'When Mr. Stimpleton's away, the Rockets will use his pool!'"

Reggie panicked. "What? You wanna go swimming in the Stimpletons' pool?"

"You bet!" said Ray. "Will you do me a favor and grab my old surf trunks?" he asked. "I think they're in the laundry down in the basement," he said as he turned to walk away.

Reggie quickly opened the basement door a crack and reached her hand in. Otto, Sam, and Twister were on the other side. Otto saw Ray's surf trunks floating in the water. He grabbed them and handed them to Reggie.

"Here they are, Dad!" said Reggie.

"I gotta fix that dryer someday," said Ray. "These are sopping wet."

SPLASH!

"What was that?" asked Ray.

"I didn't hear anything," said Reggie.

"Then we better get your ears checked," said Ray.

Reggie smiled. "Okay! Good idea! Let's go to the ear doctor right now!"

SPLASH!

Ray laughed, "Hey, it sounds like Otto is already over at Stimpleton's pool."

🚀 🚀 🚀

Several miles away, Mr. and Mrs. Stimpleton were still on Highway 1. Mr. Stimpleton was very nervous. "Violet, we have to go home!" he said.

"Why? What's the matter now?" asked Mrs. Stimpleton.

"I forgot to tell Reggie about the garage door," said Mr. Stimpleton.

"You *told* her about the garage door."

Mr. Stimpleton tried to think of another reason to go back. "But, I forgot to tell her about the driveway."

"You told her everything, Merv! In fact, you told her ten times!"

"I need to tell her eleven times! We're going back!" said Mr. Stimpleton.

And with that, he turned the car around and headed toward home.

🚀 🚀 🚀

Meanwhile, Otto, Twister, and Sam had managed to swim their way out of the basement and were standing at the Stimpletons' pool computer.

"Sam, you gotta get the water back in the pool!" cried Otto.

"I know! I know!" said Sam.

"Hurry up!" said Twister.

Sam stared hard at the computer controls. "I hope this works!" he said.

"It *has* to!" cried Twister.

Sam quickly typed on the keyboard. "Here goes." They all looked at the hose that they had put in the pool. Nothing happened. Suddenly the backyard sprinkler came on.

"Try something else!" shouted Otto.

Sam tried a different computer command.

This time the pool lights started to blink. Then the garage door started to open and close. So Sam tried something else. That's when the music came on—louder than ever!

Back in the Rockets' house, Ray grabbed a towel and headed toward the back door. "Sounds like Otto and the guys are really having fun! Let's get over there and join them!"

Reggie was still trying to stop her dad

from discovering the empty pool. "When did you eat last, Dad?" she asked.

"I had a hot dog about twenty minutes ago," said Ray. "Why?"

"Remember the old saying," said Reggie. "'To make your swim-time fun complete, wait an hour after you eat!'"

"The longest I ever waited was twenty seconds," said Ray as he crossed the driveway. "You know, this reminds me of my old pool-hopping days."

Reggie grabbed her father by the arm. "I've never heard about your old pool-hopping days, Dad! It sounds amazing. Tell me about them. Please?"

Ray stopped and smiled. "Well, it happened a long time ago in a pool far, far away. It was a hot summer night. Tito and I hopped over the fence at the Beverly Hills Hotel. It was the fanciest hotel in town! They had the biggest, most beautiful pool in the world. Some famous people were having a big old pool party. There were TV stars, movie stars, and famous singers everywhere! We snuck in, and I climbed up on the high dive. Then I did the world's greatest cannonball! I got thirty people wet!"

Reggie laughed. "Wow, Dad! *Then* what happened?"

Ray sighed. "I was banned for life. They never did let me go back into that hotel."

"You were radical, Pop," said Reggie.

"*Were?*" asked Ray with a smile. "What do you mean *were?* Just watch me, Rocket girl, you ain't seen nothing yet!"

Ray started to run toward the Stimpletons' backyard. Reggie ran after him as fast as she could. "Wait! Dad! Tell me another story! A long one! Please!"

But it was too late. He was gone! Reggie could see him opening the gate to the Stimpletons' yard.

chapter 5

Sam was typing frantically at the computer. "This better work!" he said. "I can't think of anything else to do!"

Otto and Twister were leaning over the pool edge watching the hose.

Suddenly water came gushing out and began to fill the pool. Back in the Rockets' basement, the water began to go down.

"Way to go, Squid-man!" shouted Otto and Twister.

Just then Ray was almost in the Stimpletons' yard, but Reggie ran up behind him and grabbed him before he saw the empty pool. "Dad! You really should shower before you go in Stimpleton's pool. That's one of his rules."

Ray smiled. "Stimpleton's about a million miles away by now." Then he turned around and headed for the pool.

"Oh, I am such toast," Reggie whispered, her head in her hands.

But the pool was filled with water. Sam had filled it in ten seconds!

"Hi, Pop!" said Otto.

"Hey, Otto! How about a good old family swim party?" asked Ray.

"Sorry, Dad. We gotta go," said Otto, jumping on his skateboard.

"Yeah, later, Raymundo," said Twister.

"Nice seeing you again, sir," said Sam.

Ray turned to Reggie. "How about you, Reg? Care to swim with your old man? I'll teach you how to do the ultimate cannonball."

Otto grabbed Reggie and whispered something in her ear.

"Sorry, not today, Dad. I'll take a rain check," she said.

And with that, Otto, Reggie, Twister, and Sam disappeared down the driveway.

Ray tossed his towel onto a chair. "Okay, catch you later." Then he got a good running start and jumped high into the air. He grabbed his knees and—*SPLASH!*—he executed a perfect cannonball.

When Ray swam to the surface, he saw a lava lamp floating next to him in the pool.

What is Stimpleton doing with a lava lamp in his pool? he thought to himself.

Then Ray watched as other objects

started to float to the surface of the pool. A plastic nutcracker popped up next to him. And a coconut. And a tiki torch.

"Wait a minute! That's *my* nutcracker! And *my* coconut!" Ray looked around and saw hundreds of things from his basement floating around him. "What is going on?"

On the other side of the hedge, Otto, Sam, Twister, and Reggie were watching.

"This looks bad," said Reggie.

"So does *that!*" said Twister pointing to the Stimpletons' driveway where the Stimpletons were pulling up in their car!

"Merv Stimpleton, you are a crazy old man!" said Mrs. Stimpleton. "I am not getting out of this car! Go check your silly old pool. I'm waiting here!"

"Fine, I just have to double-double check the computer system backup in case it snows!" he said.

When Mr. Stimpleton walked into his

backyard, he couldn't believe his eyes. There was Ray Rocket floating in *his* pool! "Rocket! What are you doing in my pool?"

"The backstroke," said Ray.

Then Mr. Stimpleton saw the coconut and all of the other things floating in his pool.

"And what is all that junk doing in there with you?" demanded Mr. Stimpleton.

"It's not *junk,* it's my stuff!" said Ray.

"I don't care whose stuff it is! What's it doing in my pool?"

"Well, it looks like it's kind of floating," said Ray.

"You'd better explain yourself, Rocket!" demanded Mr. Stimpleton.

Ray shook his head, "I can't explain this, but I think there's someone around here who can."

Mr. Stimpleton and Ray looked at each other and suddenly it all made sense.

"REGGIE!" they shouted together.

Next door, in the driveway, Reggie and the guys were listening.

"Reggie," said Otto. "I don't know about you, but I think this would be the perfect time to take a trip to the beach for a swim."

Reggie nodded. "Sounds good to me. Especially since I have a feeling this will be the last swim I'll be allowed to take for a very, very long time!"

okay, Rocket Power fans,
——— here's a sneak peek at ———
digest novel #2, *surf's up*,
a totally gnarly book:

It wasn't long before Otto and Twister were standing at the water's edge.

"So, we're really gonna do this?" Twister asked meekly. He was nervous, but he couldn't let his best friend go out in the water by himself.

"Don't be a wuss," Otto replied. "Just pretend you're taking a bath in a really big tub! You gotta go with the flow!"

Reggie and Sam came back to watch the pair from the sand dune. The storm was now howling along the beach.

"I knew we should have gone inside," Reggie said.

"Ah-choo!" Sam sneezed. "We still can," he said, sniffling.

"Yeah," Reggie said, "but if anything

happens to those guys, I want to be there for them."

Otto and Twister were moving along the water's edge with their surfboards. Twister was walking slowly behind Otto, his steps becoming more and more hesitant.

Otto gave his friend a disdainful look. "Twist, these are the kind of waves you dream about," he called. "Now, let's move!"

Otto ran into the violent surf and threw himself onto his surfboard. He began to paddle out toward the crashing waves, glancing back to make sure that Twister was close behind.

Twister sighed and began paddling his own board across the water. "Oh, man," he muttered worriedly. "This is like, totally bogus!"

"See ya in the lineup!" Otto called as he struggled forward. "Come on, Twist! This is it! Paddle, baby, paddle!"

Twister closed his eyes and paddled frantically, trying to keep pace with Otto. "I promise if I make this wave, I won't talk back to my teachers," he mumbled heavenward. "I won't talk back to Lars. I won't talk back to Officer Shirley. I won't even talk back to the movie screen, no matter how bad the flick is!"

Twister opened his eyes in time to see Otto hop to his feet on his surfboard. Behind them the dark green wave began to grow.

From the safety of their dune, Sam and Reggie stared at the size of the wave.

"That's a b-b-big one," Sam stammered.

"Totally," Reggie agreed.

Back on the water Otto stole a glance at Twister. Otto was trying to flash a confident smirk, but Twister could tell that his friend was scared.

Twister, on the other hand, had no heroic illusions. He was terrified.

The two friends stared at each other. What each of them saw in the other's eyes was fear.

"AHHHHHHHHHHHHHHHHH!" they screamed in unison.